Goldilocks
and the
Three Bears

and me!

For Peter – E. B.

First published 2019 by Nosy Crow Ltd

The Crow's Nest, 14 Baden Place

Crosby Row, London SE1 1YW

www.nosycrow.com

ISBN 978 1 78800 3001 (HB)

ISBN 978 1 78800 3018 (PB)

Nosy Crow and associated logos are trademarks

and/or registered trademarks of Nosy Crow Ltd

Text © Nosy Crow 2019

Illustrations © Ed Bryan 2019

The right of Ed Bryan to be identified as the

illustrator of this work has been asserted.

A CIP catalogue record for this book is available from the British Library.

Printed in China

Papers used by Nosy Crow are made from wood grown in

sustainable forests.

1 3 5 7 9 8 6 4 2 (HB)

1 3 5 7 9 8 6 4 2 (PB)

Goldilocks
and the
Three Bears

 nosy crow

Illustrated by
Ed Bryan

Once upon a time, there was a little girl called Goldilocks. She was clever and brave and usually good, but she didn't **always** do exactly as she was told.

Goldilocks lived with her mother and father
in a little house at the edge of a forest.

One morning, they all went into the forest to collect berries for their breakfast pancakes.

"Don't go too far, Goldilocks," said her mother. But . . .

Goldilocks loved exploring, and soon she spotted a butterfly and chased after it, deeper and deeper into the forest . . .

At the other edge of the forest, three bears lived together in a cosy cottage.

That morning, Daddy Bear had made porridge for breakfast, but it was too hot to eat right away, so the three bears decided to go for a walk in the woods while their porridge cooled.

Not far away, Goldilocks was well and truly lost. She was just wondering how she would ever find her way home when she saw a cosy cottage that she'd never seen before.

"I wonder who lives here?" thought Goldilocks. "I'm sure no one will mind if I just peek inside."

And in she went . . .

Goldilocks was feeling hungry, and she could smell something delicious. In the kitchen, she found three bowls of porridge. "I'm sure no one will notice if I just eat a little bit," she thought to herself.

Goldilocks tried the first bowl of porridge, but it was too hot.

The second bowl
of porridge was
too cold.

And the third bowl
of porridge was . . .
just right.

So Goldilocks
ate it all up!

Feeling full, Goldilocks thought she would explore more of the cosy cottage. In the living room, she saw three chairs.

"I wonder who sits in these chairs?" thought Goldilocks. Goldilocks sat in the first chair, but it was too high.

The second chair
was too low.

And the third
chair was . . .
just right.

Goldilocks rocked
and rocked
until suddenly . . .

CRASH!

The chair fell
to pieces!

"Oh dear!"
cried Goldilocks.

Goldilocks decided to explore upstairs,
where she found three beds.

Goldilocks **jumped** on the first bed, but it was too hard.

The second bed was too soft.

And the third
bed was . . .

just right.

All the jumping had made Goldilocks feel quite tired, so she decided to have a little nap. The little bed was so warm and cosy that soon she fell fast asleep.

Little did Goldilocks know
that the cosy cottage belonged
to the three bears.

And they were on their
way home . . .

When the three bears arrived home, they were surprised to find the door wide open.

In the kitchen, the bears saw their bowls of porridge.

"Someone's been eating my porridge!" said Daddy Bear.

"Someone's been eating my porridge!" said Mummy Bear.

"Someone's been eating **my** porridge," said Little Bear, "and they've eaten it **all** up!"

The three bears went into the living room,
only to find that somebody
had been there too.

"Someone's been
sitting in my chair!"
said Daddy Bear.

"Someone's been
sitting in MY chair!"
said Mummy Bear.

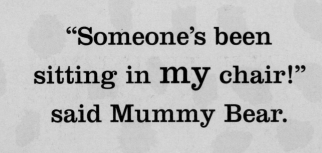

"Someone's been sitting in **my** chair," said Little Bear, "and they've **broken** it!"

The three bears went upstairs into the bedroom.

"Someone's been jumping on my bed!" said Daddy Bear.

"Someone's been jumping on **my** bed!" said Mummy Bear.

"Someone's been jumping on my bed," said Little Bear, "and . . .

she's sleeping there now!"

Goldilocks woke up with a jump, only to see
the **three bears** staring down at her!

"Bears!" cried Goldilocks.

She leaped out of bed,
ran down the stairs
and out of the door
of the cosy cottage.

Goldilocks ran and ran, and she
didn't stop until she had run all the way
back to her little house at the edge of the forest.

After that, Goldilocks **always**
did exactly as she was told.

And they all lived **happily** ever after.